The Lion Is No Longer King

Story by In Koli Bofane
Art by Lev

Annick Press
Toronto • New York

A long time ago the lion declared himself king of beasts.

His roar terrorized the savannah. Every morning at Royal Shower Time the entire animal population had to pay its respects to His Majesty. No one dared not show up.

The mongoose, His Majesty's bodyguard, had to keep watch and protect the palace night and day against snakes, since she was the only fearless one.

Of course, His Majesty the King did not fear anyone or anything, but, as we all know, a snake is a snake!

The King ruled.

The giraffes, with their long necks, had the job of pruning the trees. Since the entire savannah was the King's garden, the giraffes had no rest.

The hyenas cleaned the kitchen. Since the King was always eating, the hyenas had no time off.

The poor hippos were only allowed to stay in the pond an hour at a time so that the water would stay clean for his Majesty's bath.

"Zebra!" ordered the King, "lie down at my feet so I can eat you! It's an honour to be eaten by the king. Tomorrow I'll have Springbok!"

In other words, the lion was powerful—too powerful.

One morning, the mongoose slept in. The bright sunshine and the babbling of the stream convinced her to stay in bed and have a well-deserved rest.

"I won't answer today's calls, I'll just take a day off," thought the mongoose. "I don't care if the King is unhappy. After all, I kill snakes, I'm fearless. The King is a tyrant."

Just at that moment the crocodile knocked on
the door. (They often went to work together.) That
morning the mongoose's happy mood persuaded
the crocodile to stay and play instead.

All the other animals were assembled in groups
in front of the King, waiting for his orders.

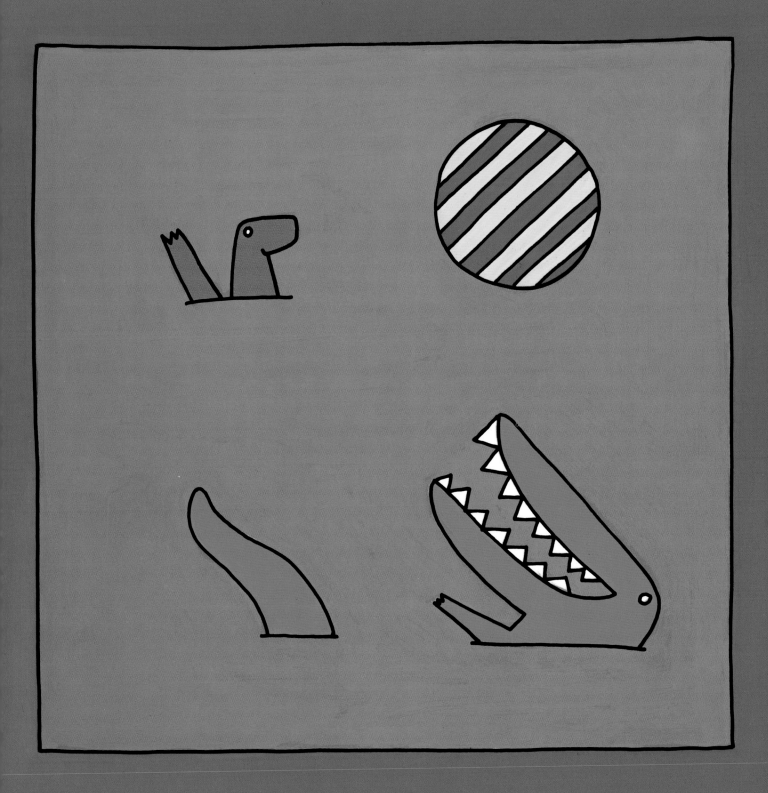

Monkeys, gazelles of all sizes, wild boar, buffalo, birds—everyone was lined up in front of the King, trying to look their best. The sun was rising on the vast plain.

With a severe look, the lion watched his subjects and felt satisfied. But just at that moment a movement in the grass attracted his attention, and a snake appeared next to the throne...

"Guards!" roared the lion. "A snake! Who allowed a snake to come near my royal paws? This is an outrage! Mongoose! Where is the mongoose?"

The animals were so frightened that they ran for their lives. When the King finally calmed down, all the animals had disappeared except for two birds high in a tree, one stubborn buffalo and the turtle, wisely hiding in her shell.

"The mongoose shall be punished," growled the King. "Birds! Come here! Fly and tell her to come here at once. Buffalo! You are strong! Run! If she dares to resist, tie her up and bring her here. Turtle! You are wise! Go and find out what she's up to."

While the King was pondering his vengeance, the clever mongoose was organizing her defence. "The King will never leave me in peace, that's for certain! I'll never be free and we all will have to go on serving him." The clever mongoose was sly as well: "Everyone knows I can kill snakes. The King must be made to believe that I am able to kill lions as well! Then everyone will be free of this tyrant."

The clever mongoose was not only sly but also quite skilful. She started to weave coconut fibres...

Later, the birds landed in Mongoose's house while she was having a meal.

"You must be exhausted!" said Mongoose to the birds. "Have some fruit. I am quite busy hunting lions around here. Look at my beautiful lion skins."

"Oh!" sang the birds, so frightened that they flew away, forgetting the fruit. "The mongoose has killed lions! The mongoose has killed lions!"

The buffalo arrived.

"The trip must have tired you out," the mongoose said. "Sit down and have some sugar cane. You may tell the King that I am quite busy tanning lion skins."

The buffalo was so surprised that he forgot the sugar cane and ran back to tell the King—and everyone on his way—the unbelievable news.

The turtle, arriving at the mongoose's house, had already heard about it. "Is it true that you killed lions from this neighbourhood?" asked the turtle.

"Of course not! I made these lion skins by weaving coconut fibres," said the mongoose. "But please say that you have seen genuine tanned lion skins. I won't spend time killing snakes for His Majesty any longer. Just imagine how happy we could all be if we could play, swim, and share a meal in the shade whenever we felt like it..."

The turtle thought that the mongoose was quite right. And while she was wandering back to the King's palace, word of the mongoose's invincibility had already spread around.

The turtle confirmed what the birds and the buffalo had already reported. "His Majesty, the mongoose is rebellious and challenges you just like other lions around here."

"But this is impossible!" roared the lion. "I'll have to take severe measures and be pitiless!"

That night the lion had nightmares. In the morning he felt too weak to roar.

The palace was deserted except for the turtle, who did not fear for her life, as she was quite small and not worth eating. "Sir, I think you should take a look at what's going on in the mongoose's house," she said.

The lion raced across the deserted plain and soon arrived at the mongoose's house. Hidden behind a baobob tree, the lion could see the coronation of the mongoose.

"Shy Antelope, fearful Zebra, you won't ever have to be the lion's dessert! You, buffalo and hippos, may go and play in the water! You, giant giraffes, the leaves on the trees are for you! From now on, the savannah is for all of us!" said the mongoose.

The lion was no longer king of beasts. From that day on he has had to get his own meals, just as you and I do.

THE END ·

©1996 R
©1997 A
Original e
published
63 rue Ch

Annick Pre
All rights r   may be
reproduced   mechanical –
without the

Canadian C
  Bofane,
    The lio

  North Am
  ISBN 1-55

  I. Lev. II. T

  PZ7.B46Li

Distributed in   U.S.) Ltd.
Firefly Books
3680 Victoria
Willowdale, O
M2H 3K1

Printed in Belgi